Please, Mom!

Written by Julie Ellis

Illustrated by Andy Hammond

"Look, rolls!
I love rolls.
Please, Mom! Please, Mom!
Can I have a roll?"

"Sh!" said Mom.

"Now, what did I want?"

"Look, cupcakes!
I love cupcakes.
Please, Mom! Please, Mom!
Can I have a cupcake?"

"Sh!" said Mom.

"Now, what did I want?"

"Look, cookies!
I love cookies.
Please, Mom! Please, Mom!
Can I have a cookie?"

"Sh-sh!" said Mom.

"Now, what did I want?"

"**PLEASE**, Mom! **PLEASE**, Mom!"

"Oh, all right," said Mom.
"Please, can I have some bread...

and a roll, **and** a cupcake,
and a cookie?"